PSYCH-OUT!

BY KENNY ABDO

ILLUSTRATED BY BOB DOUCET

magic wagon

visit us at www.abdopublishing.com

Published by Magic Wagon, a division of the ABDO Group,
PO Box 398166, Minneapolis, Minnesota 55439. Copyright © 2014
by Abdo Consulting Group, Inc. International copyrights reserved in all
countries. All rights reserved. No part of this book may be reproduced
in any form without written permission from the publisher.

Calico Chapter Books™ is a trademark and logo of Magic Wagon.

Printed in the United States of America, North Mankato, Minnesota.
062013
092013

Text by Kenny Abdo
Illustrations by Bob Doucet
Edited by Karen Latchana Kenney
Cover and interior design by Colleen Dolphin, Mighty Media, Inc.

Library of Congress Cataloging-in-Publication Data
Abdo, Kenny, 1986-
  Psych-out! / Kenny Abdo ; illustrated by Bob Doucet.
     p. cm. – (Haven't got a clue!)
  Summary: There is a new student at school who has most of the other
children awed with his magic tricks and his claim that he can mind-read,
but Jon Gummyshoes, fourth-grade detective, is determined to expose
him as a fraud.
  ISBN 978-1-61641-954-7
1. Magic tricks–Juvenile fiction. 2. Telepathy–Juvenile fiction. 3.
Elementary schools–Juvenile fiction. [1. Mystery and detective stories. 2.
Magic tricks–Fiction. 3. Telepathy–Fiction. 4. Elementary schools–Fiction.
5. Schools–Fiction.] I. Doucet, Bob, ill. II. Title.
  PZ7.A1589334Psy 2013
  813.6–dc23
                                            2013001069

Table of Contents

The Usual Suspects
THE WHO'S WHO OF THE CASE

JON
GUMMYSHOES

LAWRENCE
"LARRY"
MACGUFFIN

AMBER
HOLIDAY

NICKY
GUMMYSHOES

ECHO
SPRANKLE

MADAME
MARLOWE

Note from the Detective's Files

The name is Gummyshoes—Jon Gummyshoes. I know what you're thinking: funny name, right? Well, that's not what I'm here to talk about. I'm here to tell you the facts. The cold, hard facts about the cases I come across day in and day out at Edwin West Elementary School.

The way I see it, trouble seems to find me around every corner. So I make it my business to clean it up. I don't need this game. It needs me.

The case I'm about to share with you wasn't my first, and it certainly won't be my last. This investigation led me to mind readers, magic tricks, and a whole lot of phonies. It tested my belief in myself, too. Luckily, I had some help cracking the case. And I found out that illusions are never quite as real as they may seem.

CHAPTER 1
Who's That?!

I pushed the dry, white turkey meat and watery, brown gravy around my lunch tray. This was supposed to be our special Thanksgiving lunch at Edwin West Elementary. The crunchy mashed potatoes and the runny cranberry sauce were mixing together. I dropped my fork into the mess in front of me and shoved it away.

The cafeteria was more festive than usual that day. It wasn't Thanksgiving yet. No, that was coming on Thursday. *And boy, will that be a day,* I thought. All the Gummyshoeses would arrive in town from around the country, including my uncle—Nicky Gummyshoes. Uncle Nicky is a world-famous detective from Los Angeles.

My mom, Joan Gummyshoes, cooks all of the classics for us: turkey, homemade mashed potatoes, and corn on the cob. My bug-eyed Boston terrier, Little Ricky, celebrates too. He eats the leftovers on the table once we all pass out in the living room. But I had to wait a few more days for that.

In school, the cafeteria walls were covered with paper handprints made to look like turkeys. The kindergartners made them the week after Halloween. The fourth graders were tasked with putting on the annual Thanksgiving play about the first celebration of the holiday.

Acting has never been my gig. My interests are in sleuthing. I'm a flatfoot, a sneaker. Whatever you want to call me. I'm an all-around detective, just like my Uncle Nicky.

The play we were going to perform was about the Pilgrims who settled at Plymouth Colony and enjoyed their Thanksgiving lunch with Native Americans. I sure hope that what they had to eat was a lot better than this slop.

The table I was sitting at had the whole gang. I looked around to get the count. Across from me was Frankie Flats. He was building a hot-air balloon out of his mashed potatoes. Down the line was Amber Holiday, my former flame. We had not spoken much since I put her brother, Donny, away for a scheme a couple months back. But that's a different story altogether.

Between Frankie and Amber was Amber's best friend, Becky Lipgloss. She was the resident pretty girl and the object of my best pal's affection. Sitting to my right was said best pal, Larry MacGuffin. He was staring not at his lunch, but at Becky. MacGuffin had not been at Edwin West too long, but we had already been on quite a few adventures together. I had a sneaking suspicion that Becky was the only reason MacGuffin came along on the cases with me.

I glanced at the tray that I had pushed away and tried not to get sick. MacGuffin finished the sandwich his mother made for him. He read the note she left on his napkin, smiled, and then wiped his mouth with it.

"What's the big idea, Mac? How come you

were smart enough to bring a lunch today?"
I asked.

"I knew turkey was on the menu. Don't you listen to the weekly menu announcement? I'm allergic to turkey, Jon. That's why my mom made a lunch for me today," he responded, giving the napkin note one more read.

"What do you have there?" I asked, spearing a whole piece of turkey on my fork. It looked like a chunk of concrete on a stick.

"Oh, nothing. My mom never packs a lunch without a little note. You know, to encourage me through the day," he said, holding the napkin up so I could read it.

I had to look past the wrinkles in the napkin and the mix of peanut butter and jelly over the words. It said:

My schmoopie Lar-bear,
Have a wonderful rest of the day.
You are loved!
XOXO,
Momsies

I looked back up at MacGuffin in shock.

"Listen, Mac," I told him, "if I were you, I wouldn't show this to anyone else. And if anyone asks if it's yours, deny it up and down the street."

MacGuffin looked worried, so he crumpled the note and hid it in his shirt pocket until he could dispose of the evidence.

"Hey, Jon! Jon! What are you going to be in the Thanksgiving play?" Frankie Flats asked from across the table. I dropped the concrete onto my tray and wiped my hands.

"I decided to sit it out, Frankie," I said. "But I will be up in the rafters making sure you all look good by doing the lights."

"I'll be playing the Plymouth Rock!" Frankie said, jabbing his fork into the mashed-potato balloon, hoping it would deflate. "I get the best lines in the play!"

I rolled my eyes and turned to Becky for at least *some* intelligent conversation. "And how about you, Miss Lipgloss?" I asked. "Who or what will you be portraying?"

"I'll be playing the role of Katherine Carver," she said. "She was the wife of John Carver.

Apparently she died of a broken heart when John died of heatstroke."

I turned to MacGuffin. "You know what you have to do," I said in a whisper.

"I'm on it," he whispered back. Then he quickly turned around and ran up to Principal Links.

"Principal Links, I was wondering, could you give me the role of John Carver in the Thanksgiving play?" MacGuffin asked.

"Not now, Lawrence. I have to make an announcement," Links responded without pausing. Links walked up to the front of the cafeteria and put a megaphone up to his mouth. "Excuse me, students. Can I get your attention, please?"

The cafeteria slowly grew silent, waiting for Principal Links to speak.

"Thank you. First of all, I just want to be the first to wish you an early happy Thanksgiving. We've had quite a few interesting weeks here at Edwin West Elementary. Thanksgiving is a day to celebrate what we are thankful for," Links said and then pointed at a tray in front of a kid. "We can be thankful for the food we receive each and every day. And we can be thankful for the people in our lives."

I could not help but feel like Links was leading up to reintroducing me back into the student body.

"So with that, I would like a special young man to introduce himself to you all. You may not know him, but he knows you," Links said with a smile.

I began to rise from my seat to give a big wave around the cafeteria. Just then, a kid I had never seen before walked to the front of the cafeteria. He had long, greasy black hair that looked like it took forever to style. He wore an expensive designer T-shirt with a dozen platinum chains hanging around his neck. I thought I could see an earring, too. And he was wearing jeans that looked old and ripped up, but probably cost more than my bike.

"Behold, in all of his glory," said the boy, "I am Echo Sprankle."

CHAPTER 2
The Amazing Echo

After his bizarre introduction, I watched Echo glide through the rows of tables. Everyone watched him with a combination of excitement and fright. Echo glided up to our table and took a seat between Becky and Frankie.

"Who wants to see a little magic?" he asked, looking around.

Every hand, minus yours truly's, went high into the air. Echo took the tray of muck from in front of Frankie and slid it over to himself. He waved his hand over and over again. Then—boom!—the tray disappeared in a cloud of smoke.

The smoke cleared and in its place was a stuffed pigeon. The entire table gasped in amazement. Then they went directly into applause. Echo drank it in.

"What, you don't have live birds to work with?" I asked, looking around to see if anyone agreed. No one was paying attention to me, though.

"Sorry, guy. School regulations forbid me from summoning live animals with my mind on school property," he said, taking the fork with the concrete turkey from my tray. "But if you are still suspicious of my magical abilities," he said, putting a napkin over the turkey, "let me put those suspicions to rest." He pulled off the napkin and between his fingers was a fresh, red rose. He finished by handing the rose to Becky Lipgloss, who was about to faint.

"But if you must know, guy, my talents don't end at magic," he said, holding up a red ball. He waved his free hand around it and turned it into a small cookie. "No, my talents go much deeper than that." He tossed the cookie to Frankie, who caught it and ate it immediately. "What I do best is see tiny secrets that you hide in your little minds. In other words, I'm psychic!" he said at the exact moment a spark of smoke burst in front of him. Everyone at the table clapped again. This guy was turning everyone into saps.

"There is no way you can read minds," I said, crossing my arms.

"Oh yeah? Want me to prove it?" Echo closed his eyes and put one hand up to his temple. His other hand went in the air, like he was screwing in an invisible lightbulb. "Mmm ... I'm picking up a lot of vibrations right here at the table. Mmm ... do we have somebody here with a name that starts with an L?"

Larry raised his hand, but I caught his forearm before it went all the way up. I shook my head "no" so we could see where this was going.

"Mmm ... I'm seeing something. It's a strong presence. It's an L name. Does anyone here go by the name, Lar?" Echo asked with his eyes closed.

"Yes! Larry MacGuffin!" Frankie said, pointing at MacGuffin across the table.

Echo opened his eyes, but kept his hands where they were. "Okay, Larry. I am sensing something ... a loving vibe from someone close."

Echo closed his eyes again. "This is more of a motherly figure. One who wants to encourage you throughout the day."

"Yes! How ... how did you know that?!" MacGuffin asked in pure amazement.

This was ridiculous.

"Okay, hold on a second. Echo, is it?" I said. "I know you're new here and it's hard being the new kid. We've all had to do it. I've had to do it a couple of times in the last few weeks alone! And I realize that we all have to make first impressions in order to stand out and make friends. But telling people you can read their minds isn't going to get you anywhere. Not from where I'm standing, I mean." I went behind MacGuffin.

"Anyone can just guess a name and claim that he can 'see' that the kid's mom wants him to have a nice day. It's simple logic." I finished by putting my hand on MacGuffin's shoulder. "And if you ask me, it messes with people and their hopes when you say that you can read their minds."

Echo opened his eyes again and looked directly into MacGuffin's eyes. "Does this motherly figure call you by the name...," he closed his eyes and reopened them, "Lar-bear?"

MacGuffin's mouth fell open. "Yes, nobody knows that except Gummyshoes, but yes!"

"And does this motherly figure go by the name Momsies?" Echo asked.

"But ... but nobody...," MacGuffin looked at me in shock. "Nobody knows that but you, Jon."

"What do you say, Jon. Do you believe in mind reading now?" Echo asked, with his hand still twisting that invisible lightbulb.

Thankfully before I had to answer, the bell rang for us to get back to class.

CHAPTER 3
The School's Fooled

It took a few splashes of water to the face before MacGuffin could speak normally. We were alone in the boys' bathroom, waiting for the second bell to ring.

"It's true, Jon," MacGuffin said. "Nobody but you knows that my mom calls me Lar-bear. He's psychic. There is no other explanation."

I shook my head and *tsked*.

"Poor, easily fooled MacGuffin," I said. "It seems like every week I have to have this conversation with you."

MacGuffin stopped me. "I heard he is the student of Madame Marlowe," he said. "You know, the psychic lady off of Raymond Street. She will read your future for five bucks."

I chuckled. "He could be the student of Harry Houdini for all I care. I am telling you, Mac, there is no way that Echo can read your mind."

MacGuffin pulled out two paper towels from the dispenser and wiped his face.

"But Jon, you were the only person here who knew those things about me," he told me.

I raised a finger into the air. "Yes, MacGuffin, here at Edwin West Elementary, I may be the only one with that knowledge." I made a circle in the air with my finger and then pointed toward MacGuffin. "But the school you came from, that's a whole different story."

"I don't know, Jon," Mac said. "He looks kind of like a kid from Spade North. But I'm not sure."

"Well, maybe he went by another name," I said. "Or perhaps he was friends with one of your chums at Spade North."

"I ... I didn't really have any. That's pretty much why I transferred to Edwin West in the first place," Mac said, looking down.

I wasn't aware that MacGuffin had been a lone ranger at Spade North. It explained why I had not met any friends from his old school. So I just rolled with it.

"Well at any rate, there's something fishy about the Sprankle kid. I aim to find out what it is," I said. "There has to be a trick to his psychic ability. I'll unravel it one way or another."

I washed my hands and dried them off on my pants.

"Let's dust out of here before we're late to class," I said, heading out the door.

We exited the boys' bathroom to a big crowd in the hallway. I could see Jeff Dawkins and his morning announcement crew in the middle of the crowd. It wasn't hard to guess who he was interviewing.

"Mr. Sprankle, in just ten minutes you have captured the hearts, minds, and hopes of the whole student body of Edwin West. What is next for you?" Jeff asked.

Echo looked from Jeff to the camera and did some moves with his hands. A cloud of smoke rose and out of nowhere a rolled-up piece of paper was in his hand. He unrolled the paper while still looking into the camera. He held up

the paper for all to see. It was the flyer for our Thanksgiving play.

"I will surprise you by performing the greatest trick of all during the Thanksgiving performance. You'll have to wait to see what it is," he said. Another cloud of smoke rose from his hand and the flyer disappeared.

Jeff looked directly into the camera. "Simply amazing. There are no other words to describe Edwin West's newest student. And this reporter says that no one should miss this year's Thanksgiving play. It will be one for the ages."

Before the camera stopped, Jarod O'Berry ran up to Echo. *This probably won't end well,* I thought, *but at least people will quit believing this joker is a psychic.*

"Echo! The fifth grade gerbil, Centaur, has escaped! We need your psychic abilities to help find him!" Jarod screamed in terror.

Echo put his hand up to his temple again and started twisting that invisible lightbulb. "Mmm—I'm getting a reading. Yes! Yes, I can see Centaur. He's in great danger." He twisted a little harder and then smoke blew out of his palm.

Sure enough, Centaur, that little brown gerbil, was sitting on Echo's hand.

I rolled my eyes and walked away before the crowd started heading to class. I knew I needed to investigate Echo to see if he was a phony or the real deal.

This is going to be one curious case, I thought.

CHAPTER 4
The Perfect Part

I strolled down the hall and found the door I was looking for. Then I made my way in.

"What do you know, Chief?" I greeted Principal Links with my arms in the air.

"For the last time, Gummyshoes, it's not Chief. It's *Principal Links*. Get it right or pay the price," Links demanded from across his desk.

I closed the office door and made myself comfortable in the chair opposite Links.

"I have to say, it's nice being home," I said.

"Don't get too cozy, Gummyshoes," Links told me. "I'm extremely busy and you should be heading to class before the second bell. So let's make this quick."

I sat back in the chair and looked around the office.

"I need a favor," I said, sitting forward.

"Forget it," Links responded without missing a beat.

"It's not for me, honest," I told him. "It's for my pal, Larry MacGuffin. He would like the role of John Carver in the Thanksgiving play."

"No can do, Gummyshoes," Links said. "We need to raise ticket sales this year or there aren't going to be any more plays at this school. We can't have an unknown actor taking a major role. No one will want to see it."

I thought about it for a second. "What if I got you a real star for the lead character. Would that leave some breathing room for a supporting actor?"

"You mean you can get a star to play William Bradford?" he asked.

"With the snap of my fingers," I said, snapping my fingers. "James Weisenborne over at Edwin East owes me one for a bodyguard gig I did for him when he was going by the name Jimmy Blues. He's the biggest star in the county!" I leaned closer to the desk. "So, what do ya say? Can Mac have the part or what?"

Links mulled it over. "All right, fine. You get me Weisenborne and I'll make sure MacGuffin is reading John Carver's lines in front of everyone on Wednesday."

I rose out of my chair and put my hand out for Links to shake. "You won't regret this, Principal Links. MacGuffin is going to knock this out of the park."

"Yeah, yeah," Links said, looking back down at his desk. "Just get to class on time."

I turned around and headed for the door, but stopped as I was about to turn the knob. "There is one more thing, Principal Links."

Links stopped writing and let out a long sigh. He looked up at me again and said, "Yes?"

I sat back down. "The new kid, Echo Sprankle. What do you know about that guy?"

"Gummyshoes, I really don't have time for—" said Links.

"No, please. Just humor me for a second," I pleaded.

Links pushed himself from his desk and walked over to the filing cabinets. He opened one and pulled out a folder.

"Well, Echo is his real name," he told me. "It's short for Echolas. And he likes magic. So what?"

"What else do you have?" I asked. "I mean, where did he come from? What school did he transfer from?"

Links closed the folder and put it back in the cabinet.

"Gummyshoes, I can't show you a student's private record." Links looked at his watch. "You have thirty seconds before the second bell rings, making you late for class."

"Principal Links, please!" I said. "Don't you think that it's weird that a kid is walking around school pretending to read students' minds?"

"I see a kid who has a talent and wants to make a good first impression at a new school," he said. "That's all. I know that the morning announcement team is following him around, because he makes good TV. It's not smart TV, but it keeps people entertained."

Principal Links was right. The magic shtick he did had about as much air to it as a flat tire.

But he had that camera on him. Was it just an act? Was he just trying to get on TV? I jotted my questions in my notebook—the best tool this detective has ever used when solving a case.

Links continued, "And the illusion that he announced this morning for the Thanksgiving play will most likely drive the ticket sales through the roof." Links sat back down behind his desk. "Besides, it's no different than a kid walking around the school pretending to be a detective."

If he thought my work was fake, then he had another thing coming. "I'll figure this out, Principal Links. This kid is far from the real McCoy and I'll prove it. And when I do, you'll see. You all will see. Or my name isn't Jon Gummysho—"

Just then the second bell rang.

Links leaned back in his chair and put his hands behind his head. "Well, looks like you're late to class. Again."

CHAPTER 5

Brain Psych-Out!

The next morning I found myself awake a little earlier than usual. I put on my boots and walked my dog Little Ricky around the block as the sun was starting to rise. The ground was slick with rain from the night before. Usually snow would be past my ankles around this time of year.

I dressed for school and had the breakfast that my mom laid out for me. I took two massive bites of my cinnamon toast and washed it down with half my glass of orange juice.

"Whoa, take it easy, Jonny! Take your time eating breakfast," my mom said, putting the newspaper down. I looked at the crossword puzzle she had half finished.

"Sorry, Ma. Just a few things on my mind," I said, reading the crossword upside down. "Thirteen down is *preoccupied*."

My mom put the paper down. "What's the matter, honey? You only eat fast when something is bothering you."

I picked up the cinnamon toast and examined the bites I had taken. "Just a few things, I guess. I spent last night on the phone trying to get James Weisenborne to star in our Thanksgiving play. He said he has a scheduling conflict. So I have to deal with the director of the Edwin East play and get him to let James be in ours."

I tossed the last piece of cinnamon toast down to Little Ricky and looked back up at Mom. "Mom, I think I'm doing the right thing. But sometimes I wonder if people think I'm a phony. What do I do?"

"I don't think I understand, Jon," my mom said, looking over the crossword. "Also, thirteen down is thirteen letters, so it's not *preoccupied*. It's *disorientated*."

"I guess what I'm saying is that everyone has a talent, right?" I asked. "Like, you have a talent for book editing. So you can't be a phony while doing that. And, I don't know—say someone has the talent for reading minds. Is that something you would want to be proven before you believed it?"

My mom put the paper down and took off her reading glasses. "Jon, is anyone picking on you?"

"No, not really," I told her. "It's just ... I don't think people take my detective work seriously. People would rather believe in mind readers than detectives nowadays."

My mom smiled. "Well, Jon, people have the right to believe whatever they want to believe. You are a great detective, just like your Uncle Nicky. You know that. I know that. People will come around. I promise, sweetie."

For some reason, this made me feel a little better. So I got up, put on my coat, and shrugged my backpack onto my shoulders. Then I gave my mom a kiss good-bye. She handed me my bag lunch. I wasn't about to eat the hot lunch after yesterday's disaster. I took a quick peek inside and sure enough, I got my peanut butter and honey sandwich, a bag of chips, and a napkin that was folded in half like a taco. I pulled it out and took a glance at the scribbles on the paper.

Have a great day, Jon!
And remember, believe in yourself.

I closed the napkin, slapped it on the kitchen counter, and made my way to the door. It was nice that she wrote it, but honestly, I could not risk anyone seeing that. Enough of the kids were seen with those things, and it never ended well.

I stepped outside and took my time walking toward Edwin West. There really wasn't any reason to feel so glum. The sun was out, the birds were chirping, and there wasn't a snowflake in sight. To say I was a lucky guy would be a bit of an understatement. Then I saw a bright, shining tuft of gold walking in front of me. There was only one person I knew walking around with that kind of hair, so I ran to catch up.

"Good morning, Miss Holiday. Lovely weather for a walk, don't you think?" I asked.

She looked at me briefly while still walking. "Good morning, Jon. What can I do for you?"

I kicked a rock out of the way. "You? Nothing, really. Though I could use some company for the walk to school, if that's okay."

She let out a sigh. "Sure, we can walk together. What do you have on your mind?"

"Oh, nothing in particular. I just wanted to catch up. We haven't spoken since the field trip to Triple Crest. How's Donny doing?" I asked. "Say, shouldn't he be released from his grounding soon?"

"Yes. He'll be released next week on good behavior," she told me with a smile.

"Well, that's just swell to hear," I said. "I'll be happy to see his face around school again."

"Jon, what is it that you really want to talk about?" she asked.

I stopped and she stopped with me. "I have no cards to play here, Amber. Look," I rolled up my jacket sleeves, "no tricks up my sleeves. It's just me being me here. That's all."

She looked me over and started walking again. I followed along.

"So, what's Becky Lipgloss's story?" I asked. "She have any fellas on the mind at the moment?"

"Yeah, in fact, she does," Amber said.

"Oh, really? Let me read your mind then," I said, doing my Echo impression. I put my hand up to my temple and twisted an imaginary lightbulb in my other hand. Amber saw this and tried hard not to smile. "I can see it. I feel a presence. Is it a fella in our grade?"

"Yep," Amber said, trying not to laugh.

I closed my eyes again, "Mmm ... okay, this is getting clearer. This is someone we know?"

Amber giggled, "Yep."

I closed my eyes tight and really gave out the theatrics. This mind reading stuff was so easy. "I see it! This young man has to be the one and only Lawrence MacGuffin!"

Amber let out a loud laugh. "Nope! It's Echo Sprankle."

"What?!" I said, opening my eyes. "How?! He's the biggest phony out there!"

"Well, Jon, maybe he is and maybe he isn't," Amber said. "But at least he is out there proving

40

himself to be psychic. That says a lot more than just going around saying you are detecting things."

As the sting of her last words hit me, I walked into a tree and hit the ground hard. I watched the sky spin for a few seconds and then I got to my feet. Amber was already at the front door of Edwin West.

I rubbed my forehead all the way to the entrance of the school and pushed my way through the door. The second bell for first period rang. I walked to the water fountain and took a few sips of the cold water to make my head stop pounding. At ten minutes after nine, Jeff Dawkins appeared on the screen for the morning announcements.

"Good morning, students of Edwin West Elementary. The Thanksgiving play is tomorrow! So be sure to buy your tickets while they are still available." Jeff flipped his sheet over and started reading, "Now, for a new segment that we believe will blow your minds."

In a big plume of smoke, Jeff disappeared and was replaced by Echo. "That's right, students of

Edwin West. Your morning announcements will be replaced with my new and exciting TV show, *Brain Psych-Outs*."

Uh-oh. That made my brain start hurting again.

CHAPTER 6
Chatting with a Star

The rest of the day went down like this: Echo made a name for himself as the world's greatest magician and psychic. I would have tried to stop it, but I was too busy trying to get James to act in the Thanksgiving play. I finally got the director of Edwin East's play to let James be in ours, but it wasn't easy. MacGuffin now had the supporting role as John Carver. So he could be Becky's sweetheart—on stage at least.

At noon, I decided to skip lunch so I could make a call in the computer lab. As I walked past, I glimpsed inside the cafeteria. Echo was standing next to a third grader. There was a crowd circling them and the morning announcement crew was filming the whole affair.

"Now, Petey, I am seeing something of great importance. Something you have to do after school," Echo said, holding up his hands again. "A cleaning of some sort. I see teeth and cavities. Petey, you have to go to the dentist after school today for your annual teeth cleaning."

"Yes! Yes I do! I have to leave school early to go to the dentist! How could you possibly have known?!" he asked.

Echo looked and pointed directly into the camera. After a pause, he shouted, "Brain psych-out!"

And the crowd went wild.

"What's going on, Jon?" MacGuffin asked as he walked up to the cafeteria.

"Brain psych-outs, Mac," I said, turning away from the loony business. I noticed MacGuffin staring at Becky, who was staring dreamily at Echo. "Forget it, chum. I have some great news for you! Principal Links said you could have the role of John Carver!"

This put a little sunshine on MacGuffin's face. "Really?! Gee, Jon, that is just aces! How did you get him to do that?!"

"Well, I'm about to go finalize the deal right now," I said. "I'll contact you tonight and let you know what's happening. Until then, study the script, pal. Your big day is coming up!"

And like that, MacGuffin was running down the hall in excitement. I looked back into the cafeteria and saw Echo reading another third grader's brain.

"Okay, Matty, I see a vacation for you, to a warm place ... like Hawaii ... with your whole family...."

"Yes!" Matty screamed, "We are spending Thanksgiving in Hawaii with all of my relatives!"

Echo pointed and stared into the camera. Then he screamed, "Brain psych-out!"

I turned around and made my way toward the computer lab. I peeked my head in to see that no one was using the computers. I walked in and found one in the back. With a few clicks of the mouse and a few punches of keys, I had James Weisenborne staring at me through the screen.

"Hey, Gummyshoes," said James. "What's the deal then? You said noon. It's 12:04. I have to rehearse for my role as William Bradford. I don't have much time to get my lines down, friend."

"I just wanted to check in, James," I said. "So you got the script, then? You know what to do?"

"Jon, acting is my life. All I have to do is go up on that stage and shine like the star I am," he said.

"Good. I can't begin to thank you enough, James," I told him. "You're really helping my pal out here."

"All of this is mashed potatoes and gravy, Jon," he told me. "I'm just trying to build up popularity like that Echo Sprankle kid."

I looked deep into the camera. "How do you know about Echo Sprankle?" I asked.

"He's all everyone is talking about. At every audition I go to, I am asked if I can do magic or brain psych-outs like Echo. I've lost five roles, Jon. It's really hurtin' my ego!" James typed something into his computer. "He has over a dozen videos up on YouPipe doing his famous brain psych-outs to students at Edwin West.

Here, have a look for yourself," James said, sending me a link to Echo's YouPipe page.

I clicked on it and watched the first video that was posted. It was a video from the day when Echo brain psych-outed MacGuffin during lunch. That's funny. I didn't remember a camera being there. The next video was of Echo standing in the jungle gym with a kindergartner.

"You need to behave better at nap time," Echo said.

"Yes! My mom tells me that all of the time! No one else knows that!" shouted the kindergartner.

"Brain psych-out!" screamed Echo.

I clicked on the next video. It was Echo standing by the water fountain with Frankie Flats. He put a napkin over his open hand.

"You need to take these," he pulled the napkin off and there were two pills in his hand, "after eating lunch!"

"My tummy pills!" Frankie yelled. "Only me and the school nurse know that I have to take them!"

Echo did a backflip. "Brain psych-out!" Echo excitedly howled.

I clicked out of YouPipe and sat back in my chair. I wrote a few notes in my notebook. Echo's mind reading had a pattern. I needed to figure it out.

"Word has it, mate, that Echo will be taking over the school play. So who knows if I'll even be in it," James said.

I let out a sigh and sat back up. "Don't worry, James. I'll figure this out. I always do."

CHAPTER 7

Uncle Nicky

The walk home after school was a long one. There was just way too much to think about. Okay, maybe I had a mind reader to take care of. I had dealt with worse—ghosts, comic book counterfeiters, and rock stars. *This case should not be too hard to handle*, I thought. It seemed like people actually believed Echo was a "brain psych-outer." It just didn't make sense to me.

The car parked in my driveway was a familiar one. It was one that I had not seen in a long time. The plates were from California. My walk turned into a run to get through the front door.

"Hey, there's my daring Shamus!" Uncle Nicky greeted me from the living room.

He called me Shamus, which sounded like "shame" and "us" added together. It's an old word for a detective that Uncle Nicky taught me.

"Howdy do, Uncle Nicky. What's the lowdown?" I asked.

Uncle Nicky was tall—taller than most adults I knew. And I had never seen him without a three-piece pinstripe suit on. When he walked into a room, he made sure to take off his overcoat and hat, to reveal neat, slicked-back hair.

"The high and low of a situation I had with a croaker ended with me telling the dork to go climb up his own thumb," he said, opening his brown leather briefcase. I had no idea what he had just said.

"Of course," I said, trying to keep up.

Uncle Nicky turned around and handed me a small box wrapped in old, faded newspaper.

"Sorry for the wrap job, kid. I had to do it on the lam or I wouldn't have shown up until Christmas," Uncle Nicky said. He watched me undo the newspaper.

Inside the wrapping and tape was a small, brown magnifying glass. The handle was plastic and on the side it said "Nicky."

"I used this on my first case. Do you remember?" he asked, taking a seat in the reclining chair. "I've told you this story millions of times."

"Sure, Uncle Nicky," I said. "You and Aunty Lillian solved the case of the missing family member in New York. He was a thin man or something. You made some money on it."

"Large money, kid. Twenty large, actually," he told me.

"This is great, Uncle Nicky, honest. I love it," I said, examining the small magnifying glass.

"What's the matter, Shamus? You usually love getting my detective gear. Aren't you still using the notebook I gave you?" he asked.

"Sure. Yeah, I still use it." I let out a sigh. "But I'm starting to wonder what's the use anymore."

Uncle Nicky sat up in the chair. "Well that's no way to think, kid. What's eatin' ya?"

"Uncle Nicky, why are we detectives?" I asked, looking down at the ground. "I always thought I was a detective because I can feel it run through my body. I know I should be doing it, taking cases and helping people through tough times. But every time I do, something bad happens.

"Lately, it just seems like everyone would rather trust some mystical yahoo who promises that he can read minds." I said. "They want that more than a person who is willing to look for real clues and come to conclusions from them. That's basically what this psychic at school is doing, but he's lying to people. And he gets the popularity and the glory because he dresses like a clown and can make smoke appear at random times. It just doesn't seem right. None of it does."

Uncle Nicky crossed one leg over the other and thought for a second. He took a pen from his jacket pocket and tapped it on his knee a few times. He always did that when he was coming up with something to say. He stopped with the pen, put it back in his jacket pocket, and uncrossed his legs.

"Shamus, our lives are filled with questions that need to be answered. Some are tough questions, naturally. Every person in this world wants their mysteries to be solved. That's why they will believe in someone who can promise to solve them. Some people take advantage of that and make promises that can't possibly keep."

Uncle Nicky put his hand on my shoulder. "It's up to us, Jon—detectives. We are the ones who solve the mysteries. And we do it for the good of the people, not for popularity or glory. Because in the big picture, Jon, the entire world is one big mystery." Uncle Nicky sat back in his chair.

Just then, my mom walked in with Little Ricky on a leash.

"Jon, I need you to walk Little Ricky while I go to the grocery store. I need to get the ingredients for Thanksgiving dinner," she told me.

"He's on the case, Sis. Jon is a master answer seeker and dog walker extraordinaire," Uncle Nicky assured my mom.

I put the magnifying glass in my pocket, walked past Uncle Nicky, and grabbed the leash. I stepped outside and let the brisk November air hit my face. Uncle Nicky was right. He's the best shamus around. Little Ricky led the way down the block on his leash. I pulled a walkie-talkie from my belt and held down the button.

"Mac, you there?" I asked into the yellow device.

A few seconds passed. "Hey, Jon. Sorry. I was just rehearsing my lines. Man, there are a lot of them. Frankie has no lines playing the Plymouth Rock. I guess he was right when he said he has the best ones."

"No time for that, Mac. Listen, I need you to meet me on Raymond Street after dinner," I said. "There is something we need to do."

"I can't, Jon," Mac said. "The play is tomorrow and I barely know any of my lines."

"Well, you won't have any lines if we don't do this," I said. "So meet me tonight."

"All right, whatever you say, Jon."

"Oh, and MacGuffin?" I asked.

"Yeah?"

"Bring a little cash," I told him.

CHAPTER 8

Madame Marlowe's

The night was a lot colder than it had been during the day. I had to wear a heavier coat. And Uncle Nicky lent me his hat. I stood under a street lamp, staring at the sign in the window across the street. It read: "Madame Marlowe: Psychic and Palm Readings." Below it was a neon sign in the shape of an open hand with "$5" in it.

"Okay, Jon. What's so important that I had to stop rehearsing?" MacGuffin asked, hopping up on the curb and standing next to me.

I nodded toward Madame Marlowe's shop. MacGuffin looked that way, too.

"You're kidding, right? Jon, tell me this is a joke," he said.

I did not make a move.

"You are always telling me that there are no such things as mind readers or ghouls," Mac said. "There is no logic behind this, so why are we wasting our time?"

I pulled a piece of gum out of my pocket, unwrapped it, and shoved it in my mouth. "We're cracking the case and figuring out how Echo does his...," I rolled my eyes, "magic."

I strolled toward Madame Marlowe's with MacGuffin following me. The bell above the door rang as I pushed it open, and we made our way into the shop. The walls were all painted a light purple color. Bright, shining stars were painted in white. On one wall was a bookshelf that was filled from floor to ceiling with books on psychic phenomena. On the other wall were three separate shelves that had many different things on them.

I walked over and looked at some of the materials: candles for healing, purity, and truth; pointed wands made with stones and gems; and a Ouija board. The whole place stank and

I thought it was coming from a small stick that was upright with smoke wafting from the tip.

"This place is giving me the creeps, Jon. What are we looking for?" MacGuffin whispered from behind my shoulder.

I pulled out the magnifying glass Uncle Nicky had given me. I started examining the different things on the walls.

"Answers," I replied.

I noticed a pair of eyes peeking out from behind a curtain of beads. Someone was staring at us, or trying to read MacGuffin and me. I turned my attention back to the magnifying glass and continued to investigate. After a little while I could hear the curtain's beads separating and coming back together.

"Ah, and what do we have here?" said a tall, skinny man wearing what looked like pajama pants, a vest, and a box-like hat on top of his head. He touched the thin mustache above his lips. "Do we have two fellow psychic and astrology believers looking for answers?"

I stepped in front of MacGuffin. "We're looking for answers, sure. The name is Gummyshoes—Jon Gummyshoes." I pointed behind me. "And this is my partner, Larry MacGuffin."

MacGuffin gave a little wave. "Hey."

"Ah, gentlemen, Madame Marlowe has been expecting you. I am her trusty servant, Lorre," he said.

I let out a slight chuckle by accident.

"What's so funny?" Lorre asked.

"Well, it's my understanding that Lorre is a woman's name," I told him.

Lorre straightened himself up. "Not the way I spell it," he said, while making a sour face. He turned around toward the beads. "This way, gentlemen."

We followed Lorre through the beads and into a dark room that was a lot bigger than the one we just left. This room was lit only with candles that lined every wall. Madame Marlowe was sitting at a small, round table with nothing but a cloth and a clear crystal ball upon it. Quiet music was playing from somewhere. It sounded like ocean waves crashing.

I made my way toward the table.

"Ms. Marlowe, we'd like to ask you a couple of questions. My name is Jon Gu—" I said.

"I have been expecting you, Mr. Gummyshoes. And you as well, Mr. MacGuffin," Madame Marlowe said, resting both of her hands on the table so the crystal ball was between them. "Please, have a seat."

Mac and I exchanged looks and then walked to the table. There was only one chair, so we each sat on a corner.

"Ms. Marlowe—" I started.

"Madame," Lorre said behind me.

I rolled my eyes. "*Madame* Marlowe, it is my understanding that you make a living by reading people's futures. Is that correct?"

"You are a boy of many questions. But behind your stare, Mr. Gummyshoes, I can see a lot of answers." Madame Marlowe flipped her hands so the palms faced up. "Let me see your hands."

I looked at her and then at her hands. I would do whatever she wanted just so we could move along. I placed my hands into hers and watched her close her eyes.

"Mmm ... yes. You are riddled with doubts. Doubts of people," she closed her eyes a little tighter. "And doubts about yourself."

"Yes, I do have my doubts, ma'am. But every person does, so I don't see where this is going," I said.

Madame Marlowe started breathing heavily. "My son, there is a presence. I am feeling an overwhelming amount of energy. Something or someone wants me to speak with you."

A slight wind started blowing through the room. It was like someone just opened the window, but there were no windows in the room. MacGuffin started looking around as the wind picked up.

"This spirit, this thing wants you to do something," Madame Marlowe said. "You are channeling someone. A man in your family."

The wind was heavy, almost tearing the cloth off the table. The candles had all blown out. My hat was tossed off my head right when lightning cracked within the room.

"A man," Madame Marlowe was now screaming, "named Nicky!" Lightning burst again, lighting up the room.

"She's talking about your Uncle Nicky, Jon!" MacGuffin screamed over the wind and thunder.

"Yes! Uncle Nicky will lead you down the wrong path, do not trust him," Madame Marlowe screamed louder. The table lifted off the ground and was thrown into the wall. Our holding hands were now hanging across the empty space. "Put your faith in psychic and astrological phenomena, boy!" Madame Marlowe screamed right before she fainted.

And like the snap of a finger, the wind and lightning stopped, making the room very still. All the candles were relit, too.

MacGuffin and I just sat there. His hair was all over the place. "Should we do something?" Mac asked shakily.

Lorre entered the room behind us. "Follow me, gentlemen. Madame Marlowe must recharge her abilities. She must have got a really good reading from you," Lorre said. He led us out to the shop. He made a small cough and we turned around. "That will be $5, please."

I turned back toward the door. "MacGuffin, pay the man."

Back outside, I dusted off Uncle Nicky's hat and put it back on my head.

The bell rang when MacGuffin exited the shop. "Five stinkin' dollars and I didn't even get a reading. What a gyp." He let out a loud sigh, watching his breath float up into the night sky. "Well, what do you say, Jon? Did you get all of the answers you wanted?"

I had a plan, but I needed Mac's help. We talked it over for a few minutes. Then I put my hands in my pockets and started walking toward my house.

"Get home, MacGuffin," I said. "You have a play to rehearse. And don't forget what we talked about. Find Jeff in the morning and tell him what to do."

As I walked home, I thought of MacGuffin's reaction to Madame Marlowe. He sure ate up what Madame Marlowe was feeding us in there. But I tell ya, my stomach was full of junk food. I noticed things were a sham from the beginning. It was a nice trick having Lorre look in and get our names first, before telling Madam Marlowe who her next saps were.

Lorre got a glimpse of my magnifying glass, too. So throwing Uncle Nicky in there was a slimy touch, but it worked. We were easy. We gave them all the answers they needed to feed right back to us. So the next thing I needed to do was to find out how Echo learned Edwin West's answers. And I had a pretty good idea where to start.

CHAPTER 9
Smoke and Laser Lights

I woke up extra early the next morning because I knew exactly how the day was going to go. You could say I had a "brain psych-out." Usually I took my time getting ready for school. That day I was showered and dressed before the sun poked its head up from its pillow.

On the way to the stairs, I tiptoed into Uncle Nicky's room. He was snoring like a bear with honey lodged in its throat. I put his hat and magnifying glass on the dresser. I wouldn't need them to crack this case wide open.

I laid out everything I had to do on the

walk to school. I would have enough time to investigate before the first teacher arrived. Then immediately after the first bell, we were on stage for the big Thanksgiving play. If MacGuffin played his part, the plan would work out. After I went over it all in my head, I got through the entrance of Edwin West Elementary early for the first time in my entire life.

The halls were eerie when no one was taking up the space. My footsteps echoed as I walked toward the cafeteria. I hadn't noticed, but the cafeteria was an extremely large room when there was no one in it. It was big enough for it to be pretty easy to hide a camera where no one could see it.

I went to the back wall where there were seven white trash cans lined up. I took a peek into each one and saw that they all had fresh, unused bags in them. That would not do. I turned around and headed out the back exit to the school's loading dock.

Out back, I climbed down the dock and headed for the big, green Dumpsters. I approached one, which was taller than six of me combined, and climbed up the side. I made my way to the front and tipped over into the trash from the top.

I had to do a bit of swimming, but I got my head above the garbage and started to root around. I knew what I needed was in there. I just had to look hard enough to find it. Suddenly I started to lose sunlight and I could not see anything. As I looked up, I saw the Dumpster lid slam shut on me. *Raspberries.* After what felt like an hour, I began to see light again. Then I saw trash falling on top of me.

"Hey! I'm in here!" I screamed.

"Gummyshoes?" I saw Principal Links through the garbage. "What are you doing in there?"

I sat back on a bag. "Oh, you know. Enjoying the view."

I put my hand out and he grabbed it. Then he pulled me out. I took a banana peel off of my shoulder and threw it back in the Dumpster.

"What time is it?" I asked.

"It's 9:15!" he shouted. "You're missing the play!"

I ran past Links and back into the school. I sprinted as hard I could, following the techno music all the way to the auditorium.

Inside, the auditorium was pitch black except for the stage. Echo was on it, dancing in front of smoke and laser lights. He made some motions with his hands and out of nowhere a table appeared with nothing on it. I found MacGuffin standing next to the stage wearing his Pilgrim costume.

"Did you talk to Jeff?" I asked, catching my breath.

"Yep, it's all set up," MacGuffin replied, noticing the muck all over me.

"Don't ask," I said.

"I won't," he responded. He looked back up at Echo doing his dance. "Look at this clown. He's the reason why Becky and I won't be husband and wife on that stage."

"Rest easy, chum. I'm about to change that," I said, giving MacGuffin a pat on the chest with the back of my hand. I went backstage and found the fuse box. With a few flips of switches, the lights and music were off. I could hear the crowd growing confused. So I let them have it.

70

The laser lights came on and the smoke started to rise on the stage. There was a loud pop and I was on stage right next to Echo.

"Hey, guy! Get off of my stage!" he shouted.

I addressed the audience. "Ladies and gentlemen, there will be a slight change in the Thanksgiving entertainment today. For I, Jon Gummyshoes, will be doing a brain psych-out on the great and mighty Echo Sprankle."

The audience applauded and I let them. This was kind of fun.

"That's impossible," Echo said, putting both hands on his hips. "Only a very select few are granted the ability to psych-out the brain."

"Well then, this should be easy for you. If I'm a phony, then you will remain the best." I put my hand out to the crowd. "What do ya say?"

Echo stared at me with a mix of fright and anger. He changed it to a smile and looked at the crowd. "Sure, guy. Let's see what you got."

I raised my hand to my temple and started twisting the imaginary lightbulb.

"I am feeling something. A presence. Or an energy." I opened one eye. "Or an energetic presence. You're name ... is short for Echolas."

"Yes, so what?" he said. "Everyone knows that. Try again, guy."

I closed my eyes and made like I was concentrating harder.

"Okay, I am picking something up," I said. "It's a person ... a person who claims he can read minds but who is the biggest phony of all. This person's name is Echo Sprankle."

The crowd all gasped at the same time.

"How dare you question my psychic ability!" he shouted. "It is a gift, and you're just jealous that you don't have it."

"Well, you're right about one thing. I certainly don't have that gift. But then again, neither do you," I told him.

"And how are you going to prove that?" Echo asked.

I smiled. "I thought you'd never ask," I said, putting my hand into my pocket. I pulled out a dozen used napkins I got out of the Dumpster. I held one up for the crowd to see and I read it, "My schmoopie Lar-bear, Have a wonderful rest of the day. You are loved! XOXO, Momsies." I looked over at Echo. "I do believe this is the presence you felt from MacGuffin, isn't it?"

"That doesn't prove anything," Echo said, getting red in the face.

I held up another napkin. "Petey, don't forget about your dentist appointment after school. Love, Mom." I held up another, "Matty, I hope you are excited for our family vacation to Hawaii on Thursday." And one more, "Don't forget your tummy pills after lunch, Francis." I put the napkins down and looked at Echo, who for once was speechless. "MacGuffin, if you will."

MacGuffin flipped a switch and an image of his lunch note was displayed on the wall behind us.

"You used your show as an excuse to keep a camera around," I said. "You got glimpses of these notes and used them for your 'brain psych-outs.'"

Echo knew the jig was up. "It's true," he said. "My brain psych-outs are no more than an elaborate trick to make people think I can read their minds."

The crowd gasped again.

"People! I know there are lots of questions and mysteries out there that you want answered.

We all do! But that doesn't mean someone who dresses like an alien and produces smoke from his sleeve is going to answer them," I said. "It's okay to want help from time to time when things are uncertain," I looked over at Echo. "But it's crummy when someone decides to take advantage of that and make promises that they can read the future or any of your minds."

Echo ran off the stage through the curtain. That was the best disappearing trick I had seen him do yet.

"Just because some mystical creep can't tell you what lies ahead, it doesn't mean we don't have to be hopeful about the future. Whether we know what it is or not." I motioned to MacGuffin and the rest of the cast to come on stage.

"One thing is certain though," I said, looking at the cast. "You will be thoroughly entertained with Edwin West Elementary's fourth grade Thanksgiving play."

CHAPTER 10
No More Doubts

I've heard people say, "All's well that ends well."
To be honest, I don't really understand what it
means. But like I always say, "Life is like a glass
of milk." So I forgot about it and finally enjoyed
the Thanksgiving meal in front of me.

The play had gone off without any trouble.
James blew the audience away with his acting
talents. Apparently the play broke ticket sale
records, making it the most popular show put on
by Edwin West in history.

MacGuffin and Becky Lipgloss were
surprisingly very good as husband and wife in

the play—almost too good. No one could say there was a lack of chemistry between them, that's for sure.

I don't know what's next for Echo. He ran off and I wasn't able to talk to him after. One thing I could bet on is that his TV show would be on a break for quite some time, which was fine by me. Too much of that stuff will rot your brain, I always say.

As for me, well, I have no more doubts about being a detective. And it took a mind reader to help me figure that out. Seeing that Madame Marlowe was no real psychic helped. She was running the same gag as Echo, just as I expected. Aside from the fans I could see making the wind and the cord attached to the table that flung it into the wall, I caught Lorre getting a good look at my magnifying glass that had the name Nicky on it. To think she tried to set me up against my Uncle Nicky. He's the greatest shamus in the entire world.

"Say, Shamus, I meant to ask you. How did your investigation at Madame Marlowe's go?" Uncle Nicky asked from across the dinner table.

I looked around at my family. It was a good sight to see. I knew nobody could say anything to make me doubt any one of them. Then I sipped my milk and wiped my mouth with my napkin. "Well, Uncle Nicky, to be honest ... she didn't tell me anything I that didn't already know."

X Echo Sprankle: knew that
MacGuffin's mom calls him
Lar-bear.

X Was it just an act? Was Echo
just trying to get on TV?

X YouPipe: Echo's videos were shot
from a camera that no one saw
or knew was there.

X There is a pattern to Echo's mind
reading ... what is it?

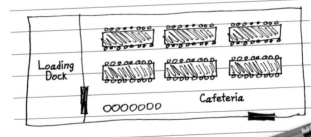